ELMER
AND FRIENDS

ANDERSEN PRESS

ELMER
AND WILBUR

Elmer, the patchwork elephant, was
waiting for his cousin, Wilbur, who was
coming to visit him.
"He's late," said Elmer. "Perhaps he's
lost. Let's go and look for him."

"What does Wilbur look like?" asked an elephant.
"Wait and see," chuckled Elmer. "But be careful, Wilbur likes to play tricks, especially with his voice. He's a ventriloquist. He can make his voice sound as if it is coming from a different place to where he is, from anywhere."

"This is fun," said an elephant as they started to search.

"It's like hide-and-seek."

Suddenly they heard, "Yo Ho! Elmer! I'm over here."
They rushed to where the voice came from.
"Looking for me?" asked a rather surprised tiger.
"Sorry," said Elmer, "we thought you were my cousin."
"Very funny, Elmer," said the tiger. "Perhaps that's your
cousin I can hear shouting."

"Help!" called the voice. "Help! I've fallen in the
pond."
"He has, he has! I can see him!" said an elephant.
"Silly," said Elmer. "That's your own reflection.
    Keep looking. He's near, but not where his
        voice is."

They kept looking and all the time they looked, the voice came from different places. It called, "COOEEE! Here I am," or "BOO!" to make them jump. It even came from down a rabbit hole. The rabbits popped out saying, "That's not funny. That's not funny at all. That's very silly."

After a lot of searching, an elephant said, "We'll never find him, Elmer. Let's give in."

"Wilbur," called Elmer. "We give in. You can come out now."

"I can't. I'm stuck up a tree," Wilbur's voice said from above them. The elephants giggled. "He's very clever," said one.

"If you don't come," said Elmer, "we'll have to go home without you."

"I really am stuck up a tree," said Wilbur's voice. The elephants giggled again.

"Elmer," said an elephant. "Is Wilbur black and white?"

"Yes. Why?" said Elmer.

"I peeped," said the elephant. "He really is stuck up a tree."

They all looked. There was Wilbur, up a tree.
"Wilbur," gasped Elmer. "How did you get up there?"
"Never mind how I got up, how do I get down?"
said Wilbur

"I have no idea," said Elmer. "But we're hungry so we're going home for tea. At least we know where you are now. Goodbye, Wilbur. See you tomorrow."

With that Elmer started to lead the other elephants away.
"Oh, Elmer," called Wilbur. "Don't leave me. I'm starving."

"Ha, ha, I was just teasing," laughed Elmer, turning back to Wilbur. "If you walk along the branch it will bend down with your weight and we can help you down." Wilbur walked slowly along the branch. The branch began to bend down. When the Elephants could reach, they pulled the branch the rest of the way and helped Wilbur off.

"Thanks," said Wilbur. "Now, where's that tea you were talking about?" Then laughing and joking together they raced all the way home.

That night, as they lay down to sleep, Elmer said, "Goodnight,
Wilbur. Goodnight, Moon." A voice that seemed to come from
the moon said, "Goodnight, elephants. Sweet dreams."

Elmer smiled and whispered, "Wilbur, how DID you get up that tree?" But Wilbur was already asleep.

ELMER
TAKES OFF

It was a very, very windy day. Elmer, the patchwork elephant, was sheltering in a cave with his elephant friends, some birds and Cousin Wilbur, who was playing tricks with his voice. The elephants laughed when Wilbur made his voice come from a hole at the back of the cave.

"It's not a good day for flying," said a bird.

"It's a good day to be a heavy elephant," chuckled Elmer. "An elephant can't be blown away."

"I bet even you are afraid to go out in this wind, Elmer," said the bird.

"Afraid?" said Elmer. "Watch this then. Come on Wilbur."

"Come back, don't be silly," called the elephants.

But Elmer and Wilbur had already gone out into the wind.

Once they were behind some trees and out of sight of
the others, Elmer led the way into another cave.
"You're up to something, Elmer," said Wilbur.
"Yes," laughed Elmer. "Make your voice come from

out there as if we were still walking away. Sound
like me sometimes."

"I get it," said Wilbur. His voice came from the
distance, sounding like Elmer, "It's hard to move in this
wind." Then like himself, "Careful, Elmer, hold on."

The elephants heard the voices and started to worry.
Wilbur called, "Hold on to something, Elmer. Look out!"

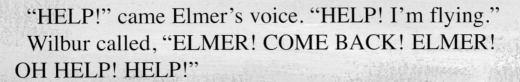

"HELP!" came Elmer's voice. "HELP! I'm flying."
Wilbur called, "ELMER! COME BACK! ELMER!
OH HELP! HELP!"

"Elmer's being blown away, we must help,"
said an elephant.
"If you go out you'll be blown away too,"
said a bird.
"Form a chain, trunks holding tails,"
said another elephant.
They crept out of the cave, each elephant holding
the tail of the elephant in front.

"Look at them," said Elmer. "They do
look funny."

"Come back, you'll be blown away,"
called Wilbur.

The elephants all started to speak at once,
but because they were holding on with their
trunks, their voices sounded very strange:

"We've been fooled!"

"The rotters . . ."

"It's an Elmer and Wilbur trick."
Then they backed back into the cave
and looked funnier than ever.

When they were safely back in the cave, Elmer and
Wilbur returned as well. The elephants enjoyed the joke
but a bird said, "That was very silly, Elmer."

"But really, Bird," said Elmer, "an elephant can't be
blown away. I'll walk to those trees and back to prove it."

"Another trick," said an elephant, as Elmer walked
away.

They watched as Elmer disappeared behind some trees.

Then they heard Elmer's voice calling, "Help! I can't keep on the ground."

The elephants laughed, "Very funny, Wilbur."

The voice came again, "HELP! I'M FLYING!"

The elephants laughed louder than ever.

"It's not me this time," said Wilbur.

"Look!" said a bird, "It isn't Wilbur."
The elephants stared; there was Elmer above the trees.
"What's he doing up there?" gasped an elephant.
"It's called flying," said a bird.
"Poor Elmer," said an elephant.

"It's my ears," thought Elmer. "They're acting as wings."
Wilbur and the others seemed very small as he flew away.

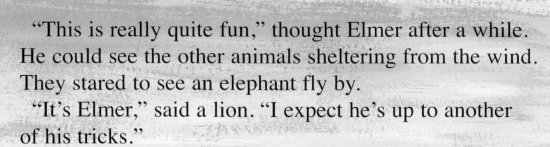

"This is really quite fun," thought Elmer after a while. He could see the other animals sheltering from the wind. They stared to see an elephant fly by.

"It's Elmer," said a lion. "I expect he's up to another of his tricks."

At last the wind dropped and Elmer landed.
"Oh dear," he thought. "It's going to be a long
walk home. It serves me right for being so silly."

When the wind stopped, the birds flew off to find Elmer and help guide him home. When at last the elephants saw the birds flying above the trees, they knew that Elmer was near. They rushed to meet him to hear about his adventure.

"You were wrong, Elmer," said the bird.
"An elephant can be blown away."
"You were wrong, too, Bird," laughed Elmer.
"It was a lovely day for flying!"

ELMER

and the
LOST TEDDY

The sky was already dark and full of stars when Elmer,
the patchwork elephant, heard the sound of crying.
It was Baby Elephant.
  "He can't sleep," said Baby Elephant's mother.
"He wants his teddy. We took Teddy with us on a picnic
and somewhere we lost it."

"Never mind," said Elmer. "I'll lend him my teddy. Tomorrow I'll look for the lost one."

Elmer went away and came back with his teddy. Baby Elephant smiled and was soon fast asleep with Elmer's teddy beside him.

The next day Elmer set off in search of the lost teddy. He hadn't gone far when he met his cousin, Wilbur.

"Hello, Wilbur," said Elmer. "I'm looking for Baby Elephant's lost teddy. Have you seen it?"

"No," said Wilbur. "But if I find it, I'll call you."

A little later a voice said, "Hello, Elmer. Where are you going?"
It was Lion.

"Baby Elephant has lost his teddy and I'm looking for it,"
said Elmer.

"Oh dear," said Lion. "Baby Lion would be very upset if he lost
his teddy. If I find it, I'll call you. Maybe Tiger has seen it."

As he came near Tiger's place, Elmer called out, "Yoo hoo! Tiger!"

"Ssssh! Elmer," Tiger quietly called back. "The twins are asleep."

"Sorry," said Elmer. "Only Baby Elephant has lost his teddy. Have you seen it?"

"That's serious," said Tiger. "The twins wouldn't sleep without their teddies. If I find it, I'll call you."

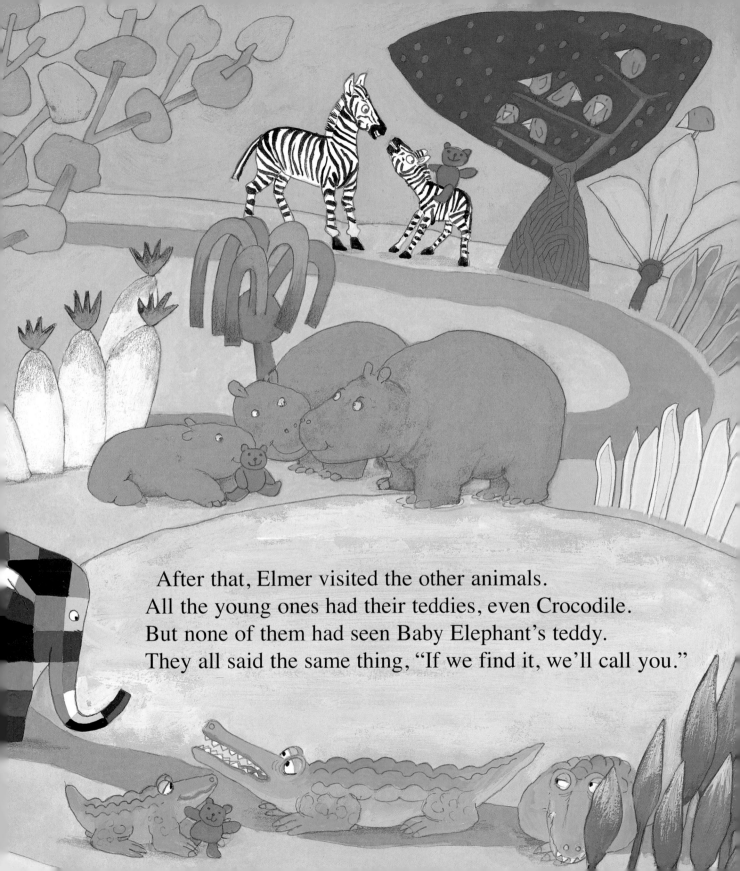

After that, Elmer visited the other animals.
All the young ones had their teddies, even Crocodile.
But none of them had seen Baby Elephant's teddy.
They all said the same thing, "If we find it, we'll call you."

It was getting late into the afternoon and Teddy was still lost.
"I hope I find him soon," thought Elmer. "It's nearly night time."
It was at that moment that he heard a shout. "Help! Help!"
And then again. "Help! I'm lost!"

Elmer pushed through some bushes and there was a teddy bear. The voice came from the teddy. "Please help me," said the teddy. "I'm lost. I want Baby Elephant."

"You can talk," said Elmer in surprise.

"Please, take me home," said Teddy. "I can't sleep without Baby Elephant."

Elmer still stared. "Your mouth isn't moving," he said.
Just then Wilbur appeared from the bushes.

"Wilbur," laughed Elmer. "I might have known it was you making teddy speak."

Wilbur chuckled. "I said I'd call you if I found Teddy," he said. "And I did. Come on, let's take Teddy home, it's getting dark."

They set off together, singing as they went.

Baby Elephant was excited to see his teddy again
and quickly gave back Elmer's teddy.

Baby Elephant's mother couldn't thank Elmer
and Wilbur enough.

"Elmer," said Wilbur, "weren't you worried that Baby Elephant would want to keep your teddy? Your teddy is very different, it's special."

"But, Wilbur, didn't you know?" said Elmer in surprise.
"You don't have to be different to be special. All teddies are
special, especially your own."

Elmer, the patchwork elephant, was in a cave, sheltered from a storm. With him were other elephants and birds. "Thunder and lightning is exciting," said Elmer. "And after the storm we might see a rainbow."

When the storm had stopped, Elmer and the birds
went outside. Elmer felt drops on his head.
  "Oh," he said. "It's still raining!"
  "Perhaps it's the rainbow crying," said a bird.
  "It's come out too soon and lost its colors.
  Look!"

In the sky was a pale shape. "A rainbow without colors!"
said Elmer. "That's awful. We must do something.
I'll give it my colors."
"To do that you'll have to find where it touches the ground,"
said a bird. "Nobody knows where that is."
"Well, what are we waiting for?" said Elmer. "Let's start
searching. You go that way and I'll go this."

"What are you looking for, Elmer?" called Lion.

"The end of the rainbow," said Elmer. "Have you seen it?"

"Which end?" asked Lion.

"Either end," said Elmer. "The rainbow's lost its colors.
I can give it mine, if we can find the end."

"A rainbow without colors? That is serious," said Tiger.

"Come on, Lion, we'd better search. You too, rabbits."

"We'll roar, when we find it," said Lion.

A little later Elmer met Giraffe. "Elmer," she said, "there's something strange in the sky." "That's the rainbow," said Elmer and he told her about the lost colors. "Can you see where it touches the ground?" Giraffe stretched very high. "No, I can't," she said. "What will happen to you, Elmer, if you give it your colors?" she asked. But Elmer was already on his way to get the elephants.

The elephants were still in the cave. "We're not coming out with that thing in the sky," they said.
But when Elmer had explained the problem, the elephants were glad to help.
"What about Elmer, if he gives his colors away?" asked an elephant.
"I suppose he'll be like us," said his friend.
"Better that than a colorless rainbow!"

Elmer was with the monkeys when the birds returned.
"No luck so far," they said. "We'll keep looking."
"Nobody can find the end of the rainbow," said a monkey.
"But it will be fun to try."

By the time Elmer arrived at the river, everyone was looking
for the rainbow. "Hello, fish," he called. "I don't suppose
you know where the rainbow starts, do you?"

"Usually at the waterfall," said a fish, "but today there's
some pale thing there."

"That's the rainbow!" said Elmer. "Come on, to the
waterfall!"

Sure enough, a colorless rainbow was coming from the waterfall. The search was over! Elmer, the fish and the crocodiles called loudly to the other animals. Then, without waiting, Elmer went behind the waterfall.

By the time the other animals arrived, Elmer was
out of sight. Colors gradually began to appear
in the rainbow.

"Hurrah!" cheered the animals.

"But what about Elmer?" whispered an elephant.

As if in answer, Elmer appeared from behind the waterfall.
He still had his colors! The animals cheered again.
"But Elmer," said an elephant, "you gave your colors to
the rainbow. How can you still have them?"
Elmer chuckled, "Some things you can give and give and
not lose any. Things like happiness or love or my colors."

Later, on the way home, Tiger said, "I wondered
if the rainbow would be patchwork."
Elmer grinned.
"Don't even think about it," said Lion. "We have
enough trouble with a patchwork elephant!"
This time Elmer laughed out loud.

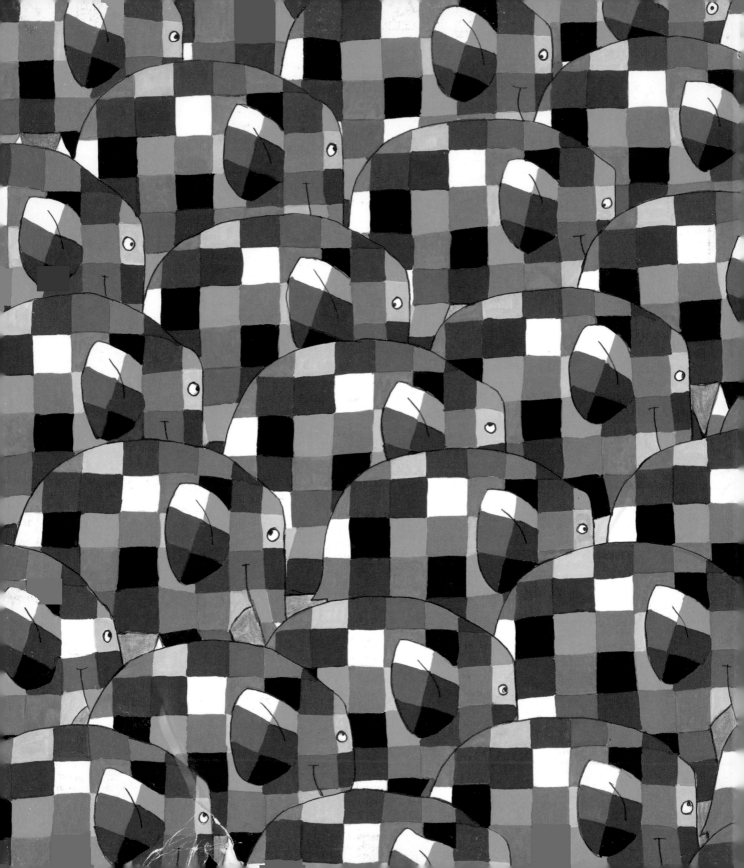